THE DOG THAT CALLED THE SIGNALS

Books by Matt Christopher

Sports Stories

THE LUCKY BASEBALL BAT
BASEBALL PALS
BASKETBALL SPARKPLUG
TWO STRIKES ON JOHNNY
LITTLE LEFTY
TOUCHDOWN FOR TOMMY
LONG STRETCH AT FIRST BASE
BREAK FOR THE BASKET
CRACKERJACK HALFBACK
BASEBALL FLYHAWK
SINK IT, RUSTY
CATCHER WITH A GLASS ARM
TOO HOT TO HANDLE
THE COUNTERFEIT TACKLE
LONG SHOT FOR PAUL
THE TEAM THAT COULDN'T LOSE
THE YEAR MOM WON THE
  PENNANT
THE BASKET COUNTS
CATCH THAT PASS!
SHORTSTOP FROM TOKYO
LUCKY SEVEN
JOHNNY LONG LEGS
LOOK WHO'S PLAYING FIRST BASE
DIRT BIKE RACER
THE TWENTY-ONE-MILE SWIM
TOUGH TO TACKLE
THE KID WHO ONLY HIT HOMERS
FACE-OFF
MYSTERY COACH

ICE MAGIC
NO ARM IN LEFT FIELD
JINX GLOVE
FRONT COURT HEX
THE TEAM THAT STOPPED
  MOVING
GLUE FINGERS
THE PIGEON WITH THE TENNIS
  ELBOW
THE SUBMARINE PITCH
POWER PLAY
FOOTBALL FUGITIVE
THE DIAMOND CHAMPS
JOHNNY NO HIT
THE FOX STEALS HOME
SOCCER HALFBACK
JACKRABBIT GOALIE
THE DOG THAT STOLE FOOTBALL
  PLAYS
RUN, BILLY, RUN
WILD PITCH
TIGHT END
DRAG-STRIP RACER
THE DOG THAT CALLED THE
  SIGNALS

Animal Stories

DESPERATE SEARCH
STRANDED
EARTHQUAKE
DEVIL PONY

THE DOG THAT CALLED THE SIGNALS

Matt Christopher

Illustrated by Bill Ogden

Little, Brown and Company
Boston   Toronto

To Melanie

ILLUSTRATIONS COPYRIGHT © 1982 BY WILLIAM OGDEN

TEXT COPYRIGHT © 1982 BY MATTHEW F. CHRISTOPHER

FIRST EDITION

Library of Congress Cataloging in Publication Data

Christopher, Matt.
　The dog that called the signals.

　Sequel to: The dog that stole football plays.
　Summary: During a crucial football game, Mike's unusual dog Harry is able to transmit plays from the ill, housebound, coach.
　[1. Dogs—Fiction.　2. Extrasensory perception —Fiction.　3. Football—Fiction]　I. Ogden, Bill, ill.　II. Title.
PZ7.C458Dn　　　[Fic]　　　82-15234
ISBN 0-316-13980-7　　　AACR2

BP

Published simultaneously in Canada
by Little, Brown & Company (Canada) Limited

PRINTED IN THE UNITED STATES OF AMERICA

Mike and his dog, Harry the Airedale, had walked from the field across the empty lot to Coach Hawkins's house. They were now seated in the living room trying to give the coach a message.

"Bad news, Coach," Mike began. "We won't have —"

"Pass it to Barker, Tip! To Barker!" Coach Hawkins shouted, interrupting Mike.

5

The coach was sitting on the edge of his chair in front of a television set, watching a football game and waving his arms excitedly.

"Attaboy! Now run with it, Barker! Run! Good boy! Five yards! Ten! Good run, Barker!"

Mike glanced down at his dog and shrugged. "We came at the wrong time, Harry," he said, disappointed.

"Yeah," Harry agreed. "But keep butting in. He's sure to hear you after a while."

"I hope so," thought Mike.

As far as Mike knew, Harry was the most unusual dog in the world. Mike had found Harry in a pet shop and had discovered that the dog could communicate with him by mental telepathy. He had brought Harry home that day and they had been friends ever since.

Mike looked from Harry to the coach. "I bet he's forgotten why he asked us in," Mike thought.

Suddenly the big man glanced around at them, and an apologetic smile came over his round face. "Sorry, Mike," he said. "But I just had to watch that play. What can I do for you?"

"I just saw Bobby Doan," Mike explained. "He can't quarterback the team in next Saturday's game. He and his family are going on a vacation."

"He *what?*" The coach rolled his eyes up toward the ceiling and slapped his knees, frustrated. "Of all the lousy luck! Well, there's only one thing to do, Mike. *You* will have to play quarterback."

"Me?"

"Yes, you. I know you don't have much experience, but you've tried hard in practice. There's a lot at stake in that game, kid," the coach said seriously. "The Number Seven Firemen, our team's sponsor, promised us new uniforms if we beat the Browns. And you know how badly we need uniforms. Ours are beginning to look like rags."

"Yeah," Mike agreed.

"I think you can do it, kid," said the coach. "Just go home and study your playbook. And now that that's settled, please excuse me."

He turned his attention back to the football game on the TV set, watched it a few seconds, and began yelling again: "Run it through right tackle, Jim! Right tackle! Attaboy! See that?" he said to Mike. "He played it just as if he had heard me!"

"Right. Well, see you at practice, Coach," Mike said quietly. He walked out of the house, Harry trotting at his side.

"He sure gets wrapped up in football games, doesn't he?" remarked Harry.

"He sure does," said Mike. "But he

lives by himself and he must not have
much company. I guess that's why he
likes getting out and coaching us."

"I suppose," replied Harry, "but he
lives almost close enough to the field to
coach us from his back porch."

They reached the intersection, waited
for the light to change, then crossed the
street.

"Harry, I can't play quarterback,"
Mike said, thinking of all the things a
quarterback had to do. "I'm a better line-
backer. I don't know a thing about calling signals."

"Well, as you humans say, it's never
too late to learn," said Harry.

"Yeah, sure," Mike shot back, and
they glumly walked home.

The Jets practiced on Tuesday, and
Coach Hawkins had Mike work out at
the quarterback slot.

He didn't do very well. Twice he fumbled the ball, and three times he threw
passes that were either too far beyond,
or too far short of, the receivers. He felt
terrible.

"Coach, I'm playing lousy," he complained. "Can't you get someone else to play quarterback?"

The coach patted him on the shoulder. "Settle down, Mike," he said encouragingly. "You'll do okay."

"Sure, he will. Except for two passes that sailed over my head he was great," Butch Stevens, the right side wide receiver, snickered.

In Thursday's practice Mike figured he played worse than he had on Tuesday. His long passes to Butch, and to Tom Reed, the wide receiver on the left side, were way off and he had trouble remembering which plays to call.

"Concentrate and try throwing shorter passes, Mike," the coach suggested.

Mike did, and discovered that he could throw them on target better than he could the longer ones. He felt a little better.

"Nice going." Harry's pleased words came into his thoughts from the sideline. Harry, Mike saw, was standing next to the coach.

A little later Mike glanced over and saw Coach Hawkins scratching Harry's head. Harry seemed to enjoy it, judging from the silly look on his face.

"I guess the coach has gotten to like the little monkey," Mike thought, smiling to himself.

"Dog, Mike, not monkey," Harry's thoughts shot back to him. "I sure hope you know the difference."

Mike's face turned red. "I sure do, and I'm sorry, Harry," he apologized.

The team practiced again on Friday, hoping to be well prepared for Saturday's game against the Browns. They had to win it, or their chance to get brand-new uniforms would go down the drain.

Mike was amused by the friendship that had developed between his dog and the coach. "I just hope that they don't start reading each other's mind like we do," he told himself. "I like Harry being special to me."

"Relax, pal," Harry's thoughts came through to him. "I have tried to talk with him. It didn't work. Satisfied?"

Mike grinned. "Satisfied!"

Harry was just a dog, but that brain of his was working every minute.

Saturday came, and Mike walked to the game with Harry at his side. In spite of the coach's telling him not to worry, Mike still felt butterflies in his stomach. Why did Bobby Doan have to go on a vacation this weekend, anyway?

They reached the football field, and Mike compared his Jets' worn, tattered uniform with the Browns' spanking new ones. "What a mess," he thought.

"In more ways than one," Harry said.

Just before the game started Harry ran over to Coach Hawkins's side and trotted back and forth with him behind the sideline. Mike laughed at the sight, and so did a lot of other people.

The Jets won the toss, and Mike chose to receive. The Browns kicked off. Butch caught the ball and ran it back to the Jets' twenty-six-yard line. But, in the huddle, Mike panicked and wasn't sure what play to call.

"Quit stalling or we'll get penalized," Butch said.

"Eighteen pass," Mike said quickly.

The guys stared at him. "What? A pass play the first thing?" Larry Curtis said.

Mike looked nervously at him.

The team lined up, and Mike called signals. Sweat poured off his face. Larry was right. Calling for a pass on the first play was stupid.

He got the ball from center, and half a dozen Browns broke through the line and swarmed on him before he could throw it. An eight-yard loss!

Mike called for an end-around run on the next play and lost two more yards. Third and twenty to go. What a lousy start!

More sweat poured down his face.

What play should he call now? He thought again of the eighteen pass play, and called it.

This time he fumbled the ball, but fell on it in time.

Frank Tooney, the fullback, punted it to get it as far away from the Jets' end zone as possible. But in two plays the Browns ran it back down to the Jets' eight-yard line. Then they tried a pass.

Mike, playing safety, intercepted it in the end zone! He dodged several Browns players, stiff-armed two, tripped over another's legs, got his balance, then ran all the rest of the way for a touchdown!

"What great open field running!" Butch cried, slapping him on the back.

Mike, breathing hard, couldn't believe
it. He had scored a touchdown!
"Nice run, pal," said Harry.
"Thanks, Harry!" said Mike.

After the kickoff the Jets got lucky
again; the Browns fumbled the ball, and
Frank pounced on it.

From the huddle Mike looked behind
him, and shook. They were ten yards
from the Browns' goal line!

He turned and looked at the ten faces
waiting for him to call a play. But what
play should he call? What play could get
them nearer to that goal line?

"Let me run it," Frank piped up.

"Throw me a pass," said Larry.

"Fake a pass, then hand it off to me,"
Butch suggested.

Suddenly all the other players tried to
tell Mike what play to call. He was so
confused he didn't know what to do.

A whistle shrilled. "Delay of game!"

shouted the ref. "Five yards penalty!"

Now the ball was *fifteen* yards from the Browns' goal line!

Suddenly a substitute came running in from the Jets' bench. "The coach says try a short pass to Larry," he said to Mike, then told one of the other players to leave.

Mike tried the pass. And it worked. They scored!

Again and again in the first quarter the coach sent in plays from the bench. Sometimes they didn't work, but most of the time they did.

Mike felt relieved. As long as the coach kept sending in the plays, the Jets had a good chance of winning the game. And earning their new uniforms, too.

Then, in the middle of the second quarter, something happened. Coach Hawkins, who had been pacing back and forth at the sideline, let out a yell and suddenly fell down.

Both teams stopped moving and stared at him lying on the grass.

"He's hurt!" Mike cried, and sprinted toward the sideline. The others took off after him.

"What happened, Coach?" Mike asked when he reached him.

"Sprained my ankle in that doggone hole!" Coach Hawkins said, pointing at a small hole in the ground behind him.

"Oh, no!" Mike wailed. Harry, crouched next to the coach, looked up.

"Don't look at me just because he said 'doggone,'" said Harry. "It wasn't my fault."

"Who said it was?" Mike replied. He looked back at the coach. "What do you want us to do, Coach?"

"Win this ball game," answered the coach. "But you'll have to do it without me. I'm going home to take care of this ankle. This time you've *got* to run the team."

Mike's face dropped.

"Mind if I take your pooch with me?" the coach went on. "I can watch the game through my field glasses and enjoy his company at the same time. How about it?"

Mike and Harry exchanged glances. "Is it okay with you?" Mike asked.

"Sure, if it's okay with you," said Harry. "After all, I am your dog."

Mike agreed to let Harry go with the coach. A friend of Coach Hawkins's then helped him off the field, and Harry left with them.

Mike shook his head sadly as he turned his attention back to his teammates. "Guys, we can kiss those uniforms good-bye," he said, and headed back onto the field. "Come on. Let's finish the game."

Within five minutes the Browns scored two touchdowns on a run through right tackle, and made both kicks for the extra point good. Jets 14, Browns 14.

In the third quarter the Browns scored two more times, but they missed the kick for the extra point once. Jets 14, Browns 27.

As his team started to lose, Mike got more and more mixed up about which play to call. He had never wished so badly for a game to end. Of all the times for the coach to sprain an ankle.

Suddenly a voice cut into his unhappy thoughts. "Mike! Hey, Mike! Are you listening?"

"Don't bother me, Harry," he said. "It's our ball and I've got to figure out something —"

"I know!" Harry's excited thoughts came through to him as clear as a bell.

"The coach got his ankle taped and now he's watching the game from his porch through his field glasses. And he's yelling 'razzle-dazzle!' "

"Razzle-dazzle? Hey, that's great! The razzle-dazzle, guys!" Mike ordered. "Let's go!"

The play had the Browns running back and forth on the field like crazy, wondering which Jet had the ball.

Butch finished the run by scoring a touchdown. Then Frank kicked the extra point. Browns 27, Jets 21.

"It worked! It worked!" Mike shouted.

The game went into the fourth quarter. Every time the Jets had the ball Mike called a signal that Harry gave to him from the coach. And almost every time the team tried it, it worked for at least a few yards.

Then, with only a minute left to play, Mike tried the razzle-dazzle again. This time Tom got the ball and sprinted down the field for another touchdown! And Frank kicked the ball between the up-rights for the extra point!

Seconds later the game was over. Jets 28, Browns 27.

"Number Seven Firemen — bring on those new uniforms!" the guys cried happily.

Butch slapped Mike enthusiastically on the back. "Thanks to Mike, our great quarterback!" he said.

Mike smiled, and wished he could tell the guys who was really responsible for their win. But he had promised Harry he would never reveal their secret to anyone.

As the Jets headed for the locker room Mike saw his dog come bounding across the field toward him.

"Harry!" he cried as Harry leaped up into his arms. "You've got more brains than a barrel of monkeys!"

"Doggone right!" Harry replied, and licked Mike's cheeks.